American Jornalero

By

Ed Cardona, Jr

NoPassport Press
Dreaming the Americas Series

American Jornalero © 2012, 2009 by Ed Cardona, Jr.

Book Design: Caridad Svich.

NoPassport Press: Dreaming the Americas Series
First edition 2012 by NoPassport Press
PO Box 1786, South Gate, CA 90280 USA; NoPassportPress@aol.com
http://www.nopassport.org

ISBN: 978-0-578-10739-4

NoPassport

NoPassport is a Pan-American theatre alliance & press devoted to live, virtual and print action, advocacy and change toward the fostering of cross-cultural diversity in the arts with an emphasis on the embrace of the hemispheric spirit in US Latina/o and Latin-American theatre-making.

NoPassport Press' Dreaming the Americas Series and Theatre & Performance PlayTexts Series promotes new writing for the stage, texts on theory and practice and theatrical translations.

NoPassport is a sponsored project of Fractured Atlas, a non-profit arts service organization. Contributions in behalf of [Caridad Svich & NoPassport] may be made payable to Fractured Atlas and are tax-deductible to the extent permitted by law. For online donations go directly to https://www.fracturedatlas.org/donate/2623

"We want to be recognized, yes, but not with a glowing epitaph on our tombstone..."

-César Estrada Chávez-

Playwright's Bio:

Ed Cardona, Jr. *American Jornalero*, a full-length play, received its world premiere at Intar Theater, New York City, May 2012. The play was also the 2nd place selection in The Metlife Nuestras Voces National Playwriting Competition, 2011. Some of Ed's other most recent work includes: *Vegi-Super-Juice*, a ten-minute play, SPIRITUALLY Blue Balled-NY Madness, Joria Productions, New York City; *La Ruta*, a full-length play commissioned by the Working Theater and currently still in development; *Jackson Heights, 3am*, a collaborative ensemble piece, Theater 167, Queens, New York City; *Who the Fuck is Nathan Hale?*, a ten-minute play, Question-NY Madness, Intar Theater, New York City; *Mongo*, a one-act play commissioned by Local 3, I.B.E.W. Diversity Conference, New York City; *Super Moon* – a ten-minute play commissioned by the FOCUS Festival of the Arts, St. Andrew's College, Toronto, Canada; *Black Sheep*, a ten-minute play developed with the Urban Arts Partnership/The New Group, Life Stories, Theater Row, New York City; *Gluttony*, 7 Days of Plays Theater Festival, Seven Collective, TheaterLab, New York City. Some of his other published work includes *Pablo's Christmas* adapted from the children's book by Hugo C. Martin (commissioned and published by Dramatic Publishing, 2009) and *Apricot Sunday*, in *2008: The Best 10-Minute Plays for 2 Actors* (Contemporary Playwright Series) by Lawrence Harbison, published 2009. Ed has been an artistic associate with the Working Theater and a resident playwright with the Hispanic Playwrights-in-Residence Lab at Intar Theatre, The Professional Playwrights Unit at the Puerto Rican Traveling Theatre, The Hall Farm Center for the Arts & Education in Townsend, VT, and is a founding member of NY Madness. Ed received his M.F.A. in playwriting from Columbia University where he received the John Golden Award for his thesis play, *PICK UP POTS!*

Credits:

AMERICAN JORNALERO was developed in part with the Hispanic Playwrights-n-Residence Lab at Intar Theater under the auspices of Rogelio Martinez and was given a 1st Staged Production by the Working Theater, directed by Victor Maog, with Jeff Biehl, Neal Hemphill, Mat Hostetler, Andrès Munar, José Joaquin Perez, and Gerardo Rodriguez. Thanks a lot for your wonderful work in the development of this play.

Acknowledgements:

Special thanks to the following for showing the Jornalero some love: Lou Moreno, Intar Theater, Mark Pleasant, Laura Carbonell Smith, Working Theater and Lisa Ramirez. Plus Mariana Carreño King for helping me with my upside down question marks.
Mami y Papi, gracias por tu amor y apoyo.

Ed Cardona, Jr.

American Jornalero premiered at INTAR in New York City (Lou Moreno, Artistic Director) in May 2012 directed by Mariana Carreño King

With
Quinlan Corbett as Toby
David Crommett as Montezuma
Bernardo Cubria as Luis
Jose Joaquin Perez as Marcelo
Bobby Plasencia as Michigan
Joel Ripka as Mark

Stage manager: David Apichell
Assistant Director: Jordana de la Cruz
Scenery: Raul Abrego
Lighting: Maria Christina Fusté
Costumes: Harry Nadal
Sound: Julian Mesri
Assistant to the designers: Irmaris Sanchez
Press representation: David Gersten and Associates

Playwright's Note:

I encourage and empower the director and creative design team to respectively handle the elements in this play as creatively as they can, using the resources available to them.

Ellipses(...) = searching/pondering the next thought/action leading into dialogue.

Hyphens(--) = cut off/rush into the next line.

Italicized(Text) = Give more emphasis/land it.

The Minuteman Project: The group describes itself as "a citizens' Neighborhood Watch of the U.S. borders", http://www.minutemanproject.com

Jornalero: day laborer, http://www.merriam-webster.com/spanish/jornalero

The dialogue in parenthesis is for translation purposes only; it is not to be spoken as dialogue.

The Latino day laborers should speak in heavy Spanish accents. Montezuma should speak in a heavy Eastern European accent. Mark and Toby should speak in heavy Brooklyn and Staten Island accents, respectively.

Cast of Characters

Luis: A thirty year-old Mexican day laborer.

Marcelo: A twenty-four year-old Panamanian day laborer.

Mark: A thirty year-old white Minuteman from Brooklyn.

Montezuma: A forty-eight year-old Belarusian day laborer.

Michigan: A forty year-old Mexican day laborer.

Toby: A Thirty-three year-old white Minuteman   from Staten Island.

Setting:

A street corner in Queens, New York, spring 2006. A tall chain link fence runs across the center of the stage. The top of the fence is covered with barb wire. At center stage there is a hole in the fence. A large stop sign facing the audience stands downstage right. The intersection is to the right of the stop sign, offstage. A garbage can stands downstage left. To upstage left, against the fence there is a pay phone. A few empty milk crates are scattered along the sidewalk, some lean against the fence. Through the fence we see elements of a worn down public playground: a swing set, slide, a space pod.

SCENE ONE: PESETAS

LIGHTS FADE UP:

Monday morning, 6 a.m. We hear the sounds of a busy intersection.
Marcelo enters on the other side of the fence through the playground.
He wears a back pack. He steps through the hole in the fence. He
grabs a milk crate and sits down. He checks his cell phone for a
signal.

Beat. We hear a truck drive by slowly. Marcelo eyes the truck. The
truck speeds off. Marcelo's cell phone rings.

MARCELO: (To Cell Phone): Hola (Hello), Rosita --
bueno (hello)...Rosita, no te oigo (I can't hear
you)...¿estás alli? (are you there?)...¿Están bien? (Is
everything okay?) -- ¿bueno? (hello?)...Rosa, muévete
a otro lugar (move to another spot)...¿Me oyes? (Can
you hear me?)...¿Dónde estás? (Where are
you?)...Tennessee...No te oigo (I can't hear you) --
Rosita -- Bueno (Hello)...Llámame otra vez (Call me
back)...Esperate (Wait)...

Marcelo crosses to the pay phone to check the number.

MARCELO (CONT'D): Rosita -- escúchame (listen)...llámame a este
número (Call me at this number)...718-347-2473...Bueno –

The call is disconnected.

He stands by the pay phone, beat. Luis enters along the sidewalk
with a Spanish Language newspaper, a tool bag with an I-Beam level
sticking out of it, and a tray of coffee. The pay phone rings.

MARCELO (CONT'D): (quickly picking up the pay
phone)Bueno...hello...No...NO --

The call is disconnected.

Hello...

9

Marcelo hangs up the phone.

LUIS: ¿Todo bien? (Everything okay?)

MARCELO: No... (holding out his cell phone) ..Estos
malditos teléfonos no sirven para nada. (These damn
cell phone are worthless.)

Luis grabs Marcelo's phone and dials his own cell phone number.
Luis' cell phone rings in his pocket.

LUIS: It looks to be working fine to me.

MARCELO: (grabbing cell phone back) ...Not when
you need it.

LUIS: Ay (Oow)...good morning to you too.

MARCELO: Ehh...

Marcelo grabs a coffee out of the tray. Luis stares him down.

LUIS: You're welcome.

MARCELO: (sarcastically) It better not be cold.

LUIS: Tú sí que eres un animal. (You truly are an
animal.)

MARCELO: (grabbing his crotch) What you want...a
kiss... (laughing)

The two settle in as they both sit down on a couple of milk crates.
They prep their coffee. Beat. Marcelo checks to see if his cell phone
has a signal. Luis looks through his newspaper. Beat.

LUIS : Diez dólares que los Mets ganan la serie este
año. (Ten dollars that the Mets win the series this
year.)

MARCELO: You are better off picking the Yankees.

LUIS: The Mets have a good team this year. You
watch --

Michigan enters the playground on the other side of the fence. He carries a tool bag.

MICHIGAN: (whistles) ...Buenos días, patitos feos. (Good morning, ugly ducklings.)

Michigan gingerly steps through the hole in the fence.

MICHIGAN (CONT'D) Ay-ay-ay, qué vejez. (Oow-Oow, old age is tough.)

He places his bag on the ground.

MICHIGAN (CONT'D) Y Qué...

LUIS: Esperando como siempre. (Waiting like always.)

MICHIGAN: Hoy trabajamos. (Today we work.)

Luis throws Marcelo then Michigan a questionable look.

MICHIGAN (CONT'D): No me mires así (Don't look at me like that), Luis. Today, will be our day.

LUIS: (purposefully) Tu café (Your coffee), Michigan (Mee-chee-gun).

MICHIGAN: Gracias (Thank you).

The three settle onto their respective milk crates. Beat.

LUIS: ¿Y (And) Montezuma?

MARCELO: I don't think he's coming today.

MICHIGAN: He's doing some work for his Super.

MARCELO: Must be nice.

LUIS: How come I didn't know. I bought a coffee for him.

MICHIGAN: You'll drink it later.

LUIS: I'd rather drink warm piss than cold coffee.

MARCELO: Well if things don't pick up you might have to.

LUIS: (to Michigan) Marcelo tiene razón, güey. (has a point, my friend.)

MICHIGAN: Luis, today will be our day, you'll see.

We hear a large pick up truck approaching.

MICHIGAN (CONT'D) (referring to the approaching truck) You see.

The three stand and eye the approaching truck.

LUIS: (slapping Michigan on the arm) I think it's Joel el Polaco (the Pole).

MICHIGAN: Te lo dije. (I told you.)

The three grab their bags. The Truck drives by.

MARCELO: Bye -- bye, gringito que no es Joel el Polaco (white boy who isn't Joel the Pole).

MICHIGAN : (more for himself) It's early.

Marcelo and Luis give Michigan the same questionable look.

MICHIGAN (CONT'D): Don't look at me like that.

Transition Lights:

Same day, same corner, a couple hours have passed. Michigan sits reading Luis' newspaper. Luis and Marcelo stand over a couple quarters that sit next to one of the grout lines on the sidewalk.
LUIS: Mine's closer.

MARCELO: No, no...
(reaching toward the coins) Look, mine is --

LUIS: Don't touch them.

MARCELO: I wasn't going to touch them.

LUIS: Michigan, which ones closer?

MICHIGAN: (without even looking) Marcelo.

LUIS: ¡Ni miraste, güey! (You didn't even look, man!)

MARCELO: (grabbing the coins) ...I told you.

LUIS: That ain't right. You need to stop babying tu Puto de (your fag from) Panamá.

MARCELO: Deja eso (Leave that alone), Luis.

Marcelo positions himself for another toss.

MARCELO (CONT'D) (to Luis) Vente, Loco...para completar el dólar. (Come on, man...so I can complete the whole dollar.)

LUIS: No...así no juego. (Like that I'm not playing.)

MICHIGAN: (to Luis) His quarter was closer.

LUIS: (to Michigan) Did you even look?

MARCELO: HE DID.

LUIS: Michigan?

MICHIGAN: Marcelo, it's been an hour.

MARCELO: Oh, gracias (thank you).

Marcelo crosses to the pay phone. He rest his harm on top of it as he pulls his cell phone out. He dials.

LUIS: (to Michigan) You didn't even look.

MICHIGAN: Tomorrow his family arrives...and then all the good graces will be on you, ya verás (you'll see).

LUIS: Good graces --

MICHIGAN: Even Montezuma will be showering you with good graces.

LUIS: We haven't worked in over a week.

MICHIGAN: New spots need a little time. And you know it's better that we moved.

Marcelo dials his cell phone again. Luis grabs the last coffee, removes the lid and takes a small sip.

LUIS: (the coffee is cold, he makes a face) Ehh...I trust you, Michigan --

MICHIGAN: It will work out. It already has -- Mira lo que nos perdimos (Look at what we missed).

Luis agrees with Michigan.

LUIS: (to Marcelo) Nada (Nothing), Marcelo?

MARCELO: She doesn't pick up.

LUIS: Maybe they're...still somewhere with no signal.

MARCELO: I'm starting to worry. She always called me first thing in the morning.

MICHIGAN: She did...it just got disconnected.

MARCELO: I told her to call me on the pay phone.

MICHIGAN: Marcelo, cálmate (relax).

MARCELO: Dejame llamar su mamá, la Doña. (Let me call her mother.) To hear the tears and worry again.

MICHIGAN: Háblale con calma. (Talk to her calmly.) -- And she will feel better.

MARCELO: I'll be down the block. Pick up the pay phone if it rings --

MICHIGAN: We will.

MARCELO: And if work comes --

LUIS: Hah!

MARCELO: Don't leave without me.

MICHIGAN: Of course. And don't go too far...because if they only need one -- it's your turn.

We hear a truck approaching.

MARCELO: I'll be at Pepino's.

The truck slows down and drives by slowly. The guys eye the truck.

LUIS: Maybe our luck has changed.

MARCELO: That *white truck* drove by earlier.

LUIS: (throwing up his hands) Cheap labor here.

The truck speeds off. They watch it as it drives out of sight.

TRANSITION LIGHTS:

Same day, same corner, a couple hours have passed. The guys sit rather dejected. The wait has worn them down. Furthermore the worry is evident on Marcelo's face.

LUIS (CONT'D) (sarcastically to Michigan)
Today, will be our day, General (Spanish
pronunciation).

MICHIGAN: ¿Qué quieres que haga, Luis? (What do you want me
to do, Luis?)

LUIS: For a week I've said nothing, right, Marcelo.

MARCELO: I don't know.

MICHIGAN: Sometimes we have to wait.

LUIS: Nunca tanto (Never this long).

MICHIGAN: I'll call Bengie later tonight, okay.

LUIS: ¿Por favor? (Please?)

MARCELO: He doesn't like it when you call him.

LUIS: He'll get over it.

Beat. They wait.

LUIS (CONT'D): Yo me voy (I'm leaving). Why stay...if no work by
this time --

MICHIGAN: (to Marcelo) ¿Y tú? (And you?)

MARCELO: (he considers it) ...Me voy
tambien. (I'm out of here too.)

MICHIGAN: Pues vámonos. (Well let's go then.)

LUIS: Maybe we should check the old corner?

MICHIGAN: (defiantly) Allá no voy. (I'm not
going over there.)

LUIS: Pero (But), Michigan...time has past. Right, Marcelo?

MARCELO: I'm with Michigan.

LUIS: What can it hurt?

MICHIGAN: This is my new spot. Tranquilo...sin problemas. (Calm...with no problems.)

Luis shrugs his shoulders. The guys gather their things.

LUIS: (playfully to Michigan) ...You're so cute with all of your passion.

MICHIGAN: Fuck off, come mierda (shit head).

LUIS: (playfully) Ay, tan lindo que me hablas también. (Ooo, how sweet you talk to me too.)

They share a laugh. They slowly begin to exit in the same direction that they entered.

MICHIGAN: Marcelo! Don't worry...everything will be fine.

MARCELO: I know.

MICHIGAN: She'll call you soon.

LUIS: From there to here...there are always times of bad communication, no. It's part of it.

MICHIGAN: (agrees) ...Nos vemos mañana. (I'll see you tomorrow.)

They exit. Beat.

LIGHTS FADE OUT:

SCENE TWO: MINUTE LABOR

LIGHTS FADE UP:

Next morning, same corner, 7 a.m. Mark stands center stage right wearing a T-shirt that reads, "God Bless America!" A camera hangs around his neck. The hole in the fence has been noticeably repaired with another piece of fencing. The patch work is a bit shoddy. Beat, we hear a military helicopter fly by.

MARK: (to himself) ...Look at that...

Marcelo enters on the playground side of the fence. He wears a back pack.

MARK (CONT'D): (to the helicopter) ...Cool...

Marcelo looks up as he crosses to the center of the fence. He then studies the repaired section. He pulls on it. Beat.

MARK (CONT'D): (TO MARCELO) GOOD MORNING.

MARCELO: Good morning.

Beat. They eye each other.

MARK: (to break the silence) It's amazing how they fly.

MARCELO: I'm sorry?

MARK: Helicopters.

MARCELO: Yes...it is.

Beat.

Marcelo grabs onto the repaired part of the fence.

18

MARCELO (CONT'D): (with a grin) Did you
fix this hole?

MARK: No, wasn't me.

MARCELO: Oh, okay --

MARK: Why --

MARCELO: Has that phone rang?

MARK: Excuse me?

MARCELO: The pay phone.

MARK: No...not since I've been here.

MARCELO: Have you been here long?

MARK: Awhile.

MARCELO: Okay...gracias (thank you).

Marcelo turns to exit.

MARK: But! Most pay phones don't take incoming calls.

MARCELO: Okay --

MARK: No incoming calls...so no need to worry about the phone
ringing.

Marcelo grabs onto the fence with both hands.

MARCELO: This one does.

MARK: You sure?

MARCELO: Yes...I am...and my worry is my worry,

(slightly under his breath) Maricón
(motherfucker).

MARK: Hey. I heard that...and I know what it means.

MARCELO: Huh?

MARK: What you just said.

MARCELO: Good.

They size each other up through the fence.

MARK: You, maricón (poorly pronounced).

MARCELO: No...you maricón.

They eye each other as Marcelo exits. Beat, we hear a truck pull up.

MARK: (to off-stage) Hey! Good morning!

Toby enters holding a small brown paper bag with a coffee and bagel in it.

TOBY: Good morning. Looks like you got some early action.

MARK: He could have been one.

TOBY: He fit the profile.

Toby pulls on the repaired part of the fence.

MARK: He did ask about that hole in the fence.

TOBY: (laughing) ...I'm sure he did. What else did he say?

MARK: Not much.

TOBY: Fuck'em.

MARK: He asked about the phone --

TOBY: You don't have to tell them nothing.

MARK: I was trying to be civil. But --

TOBY: You're stepping right in -- I like that.

MARK: I just went with the flow.

TOBY: Speaking of flow. Me and Mike did a little covert-opts last night and blocked the hole.

MARK: Really.

TOBY: Hit and run, you know. Harass them a bit. Make those free-loaders walk around the park.

MARK: That was smart.

TOBY: It was Mike's idea. He noticed that they were cutting through the park.

MARK: Mike from second shift?

TOBY: Yeah. Well, he used to be on second shift.

MARK: He was on this corner?

TOBY: No, this is a new shape-up. He was at the other corner by the Home Depot.

MARK: Really?

TOBY: Yeah. The one that got busted up last week.

MARK: Oh yeah, you mentioned that.

TOBY: It was on the news.

MARK: I missed it.

TOBY: I.C.E. rolled in and cracked some heads.

MARK: It got that ugly?

TOBY: Uhh, not really. Mike said it was pretty orderly but you know what I mean.

MARK: Yeah, yeah --

TOBY: Mike gave me a call but by the time I got there it was all cleaned up.

MARK: That's too bad.

TOBY: I would have really loved to see it go down.

Mark agrees.

TOBY (CONT'D): A victory for us. But the fight continues. And that's why you're here.

MARK: I'm ready.

TOBY: Mike had noticed that the other corner got a little lighter right before the raid. It took us a couple days to find this corner. But you look hard enough and you'll find them.

MARK: So a couple guys left in the nick of time, huh.

TOBY: They got lucky. One crew left and set up a spot here. Mike would have taken the corner but he got called up, you know.

MARK: Called up, wow...I didn't know that.

TOBY: He was kind of okay with it being laid-off and all.

MARK: I don't know. I think I'd rather collect than be shot at.

TOBY: Either way he's defending our freedoms -- he's a patriot.

MARK: Of course.

TOBY: He leaves in a couple weeks. We're going to have a little something for him -- I'll let you know.

MARK: Please do.

Toby studies the repaired hole in the fence. Mark does the same.

TOBY: Yeah, so we did some surveillance early yesterday on this corner and then came back at night.

MARK: You guys are serious.

TOBY: (defensive) This is serious.

MARK: Oh, I know. I meant it like...*Bad Ass*.

Toby agrees.

TOBY: You should have seen it. This street gets a little sketchy at night.

MARK: I'm sure it does.

TOBY: Anyway -- (hands Mark the bag) This is for you.

MARK: Oh, Thanks...what do I owe you?

TOBY: Don't worry about it.

MARK: Really?

TOBY: Yeah, I got this one.

MARK: Thanks.

TOBY: So we'll see what happens. Maybe he'll tell his friends and this corner will be neutralized that easy.

MARK: We'll see.

TOBY: But, I doubt it.

MARK: Exactly.

TOBY: You have all the contact info, right?

MARK: I got it all.

TOBY: You have change?

MARK: I have a phone card.

TOBY: Good...I'll be --

MARK: I plan on getting a cell phone soon.

TOBY: Don't worry about it --

MARK: I just haven't got around to it...lost it.

TOBY: Once our chapter gets a little more organized, maybe some sponsorship, we'll have all we need.

MARK: You think that's going to come through for us?

TOBY: I like how you're already using *us*.

MARK: Well...

TOBY: I hope it does come through, because it's about *us*.

MARK: Those Nextel phones would be nice.

TOBY: Yeah, those are --

MARK: They have both -- a radio and phone.

TOBY: I know, my nephew has one. Anyway, if anything comes up
--

MARK: Should I have taken pictures of him?

TOBY: No, it's more for the folks and contractors who pick these clowns up.

MARK: Right.

TOBY: If you see one of those commercial trucks or vans approaching -- snap a picture. I'm thinking of trying to start a data base of all our intel.

MARK: Okay.

TOBY: But, you'll barely have to point your camera at them before they speed off.

MARK: But definitely no photos of the guys?

TOBY: Not right now. That could set them off pretty quick. And we don't want to kick them in the balls too hard -- you know what I mean.

MARK: Ease our way in.

TOBY: Yeah, let the blocked fence settle in a little bit.

MARK: Sounds like a plan.

TOBY: It's tactics, you know. I mean if we could chase them out of here with bats we would.

MARK: We would?

TOBY: You know what I mean...

MARK: (bit unsure) ...Yeah...

TOBY: We can't. The legalities of this country protect everybody, you know. It's what makes us great and sometimes gets in the way. It ain't fair but you have to work in the system.

MARK: You got to do it.

TOBY: So tactics...fixing the fence. Your presence. Then we step it up.

MARK: Increase the pressure.

TOBY: Exactly. Harass them. You'll see...they're a stubborn, arrogant bunch.

MARK: I get it.

TOBY: The effort will pay off. We definitely had something to do with the raid of the shape-up by the Home Depot -- I guarantee it.

Mark agrees.

TOBY (CONT'D): Alrighty then. I'll be cruising around this morning. So if you need anything...just call me.

MARK: Okay...so where else are we?

TOBY: One spot in all five boroughs and a bunch of us downtown letting our presence be known.

MARK: Nice.

TOBY: I love the T-shirt. Good move.

MARK: Thanks, my mother had it made for me.

TOBY: God bless her.

MARK: God bless her.

TOBY: Okay, good work. I'm going to take off but I'll check in later.

MARK: Okay.

TOBY: I'm never too far away.

Toby starts to exit.

MARK: Is that your new truck?

TOBY: Yeah, I've had it for a couple of months now.

MARK: It's nice.

TOBY: I love it.

MARK: Nice color.

TOBY: My favorite.

MARK: A little tough to keep clean.

TOBY: It's worth it.

MARK: That's a 07?

TOBY: Of course.

MARK: A Dodge?

TOBY: What else is there?

MARK: (laughing) ...You said it.

TOBY: We'll take a ride later.

MARK: Let's do that.

TOBY: Do you have a truck?

MARK: I wish.

TOBY: What do you drive?

MARK: Uhh...a Hyundai Excel.

Mark gestures with his head in the direction of his car parked near by.

TOBY: ...Oh...dependable.

They both stare at it.

MARK: Does the job.

TOBY: That's all you can expect.

MARK: They got a couple plants out in the Mid-West -- you know.

TOBY: Do they?

MARK: Yeah...I'm pretty sure.

Beat.

MARK (CONT'D): I give the wife the good car, it's an Explorer, a Ford.

TOBY: Those are nice. Is it an 07?

MARK: No, 97.

TOBY: Hmm...good year.

MARK: I used to drive the Excel to work, for the commute -- you know?

TOBY: Gas is a killer.

MARK: Tell me about it.

Beat.

TOBY: We're really glad you joined on.

MARK: It's my pleasure.

TOBY: Giving of your time is a...very American.

MARK: I'm just happy I can help.

TOBY: We're doing good work.

MARK: Without a doubt.

TOBY: Alright --

MARK: So a presence.

TOBY: Yup. Just be a presence.

MARK: A presence...okay.

TOBY: Again, if anything --

MARK: So, I engage only if I have to, rather then try to infiltrate a little.

TOBY: Mark...just be yourself.

MARK: I can do that.

TOBY: For the most part we just want to be a presence.

MARK: A presence.

TOBY: To make sure they know we're watching.

MARK: Watching for what exactly?

TOBY: Watching for them.

MARK: ...Right.

TOBY: You're just a guy standing on the corner in this great free nation of ours...taking no bull shit.

MARK: Okay.

TOBY: If they get physical with you. You hold your ground.

MARK: I'm not scared --

TOBY: Hold your ground and then go into a controlled withdraw, and give us a call. About eighty percent of these guys have criminal records back home. They're a nasty bunch. So stay on your toes.

MARK: Eighty percent?

TOBY: I wouldn't be surprised. Anyway, There's a pay phone there and I think a few blocks that way... (pointing off-stage)

MARK: Sounds like a plan.

TOBY: Do you have pepper spray?

MARK: No. I didn't have time to pick one up.

TOBY: Hmmm...I have some in the truck but it's my personal arsenal...you know --

MARK: Yeah, of course. I wouldn't expect you to part with it. I'll be fine.

TOBY: I'll see what I can do. I'll ask around to see if anyone has a spare can.

MARK: Okay, thanks.

TOBY: So, I'll see you later.

MARK: Okay, thanks for breakfast.

TOBY: You got it.

Toby exits. Beat, Mark eats his bagel, he's hungry. Luis enters along the sidewalk with a Spanish Language newspaper, a tool bag, and an I-Beam level. He studies the repaired part of the fence. He leans on the fence just to the left of the repaired hole. Beat, Montezuma enters with a back pack, banana, and a Russian Language newspaper, he studies the repaired part of the fence. He then stands by the trash can and peels the banana, he takes a bite. The three exchange looks.

LUIS: (to Montezuma, referring to the repaired fence) The city?

MONTEZUMA: Looks too well done.

LUIS: Not that well done. Look at it, it's not completely secured.

Beat. They both stand and look at the fence.

MONTEZUMA: Should we call Marcelo o (or) Michigan? To tell them to go around the park.

LUIS: They never pick up their phones anyway.

MONTEZUMA: Maybe when you call.

LUIS: Trust me, I've been around them when you call.

MONTEZUMA: (sarcastically) Why you so sensitive --

LUIS: Anyway, my friend...Montezuma...you forgot again?

MONTEZUMA: What?

LUIS: The coffee?

MONTEZUMA: No -- no, it's not my turn.

LUIS: Yes it is.

MONTEZUMA: No, it's yours.

LUIS: I brought it yesterday, so don't play stupid.

MONTEZUMA: I wasn't here yesterday...and...it's not my turn.

Mark crosses toward the trash can. He tosses the brown paper bag in. Montezuma and Luis watch him as he returns to his side of the sidewalk.

LUIS: Pues, y mi plátano? (Well, where's my banana?)

MONTEZUMA: Y mi periódico? (Where's my newspaper?)

LUIS: You have one --

MONTEZUMA: Because I knew you would forget --

LUIS: I see how you are.

Montezuma gives Luis the finger.

MONTEZUMA: I got your banana right here.

LUIS: Real classy...animal (Spanish pronunciation).

Beat, Montezuma eyes Mark. Mark sips his coffee loudly.

MONTEZUMA: (to Luis) Y este pinche puto?
(Who's this bitch ass?)

LUIS: Será nuevo. (Maybe he's new.)

MONTEZUMA: Tu crees? (You think?)

LUIS: It took them longer then I thought.

MONTEZUMA: I wonder what happened to the other guy.

LUIS: Maybe he got promoted to Manhattan.

MONTEZUMA: I won't miss him --

LUIS: He was too serious.

MONTEZUMA: A bit of a bore.

LUIS: But at least we knew his stares.

MONTEZUMA: What was his name?

LUIS: Daulton?

MONTEZUMA: I don't think so.

LUIS: Dick?

MONTEZUMA: Like pito (Prick)?

LUIS: No, like Dick Clark...Moby Dick -- Cheney.

MONTEZUMA: I don't think that's it.

Mark reaches into his back pocket and pulls out an English to Spanish dictionary, he tries to hide it from the others.

MONTEZUMA (CONT'D): (referring to Mark) No parece uno de ellos. (He doesn't look like one of them.)

LUIS : (sarcastically) Maybe another you buscando trabajo (looking for work).

MONTEZUMA: No -- no...he looks to...frágil (fragile) to be one of me.

LUIS: Well, he's not one of me.

Montezuma and Luis both study Mark closely.

MONTEZUMA: (to Luis) Polaco (Polish).

LUIS: Puede ser Ruso. (He can be Russian.)

MONTEZUMA: Eslovaquia. (Slovakia.)

They study Mark.

MONTEZUMA (CONT'D): Rumania. (Romania.)

LUIS: Lituania. (Lithuania.)

MONTEZUMA: (studying Mark) ...De (From)
one of the Stan's.

LUIS: ¿Qué? (What?)

MONTEZUMA: Kazakhstan, Kyrgyzstan, Uzbekistan.

LUIS: Oh, si (yeah).

MONTEZUMA: Turkmenistan.

LUIS: Okay.

MONTEZUMA: Tajikistan.

LUIS: Basta, hombre. Vele la cara, ese es un gringo no un terrorista.
(Enough, man. Just look at his face, he's a white boy not a terrorist.)

MONTEZUMA: Terrorist can be any shape or color.

LUIS: Whatever...but seriously...¿Y mi café, hombre? (Where's my
coffee, man?)

MONTEZUMA: Ask Michigan or Marcelo when they get here, I
brought the coffee the other day.

Beat.

LUIS: (studying Mark) ...Ese loco es Ruso. (That nut is
Russian.) (extends his hand to seal the bet) ...¿Diez
dólares a que es Ruso? (Ten dollars that he's Russian?)

MONTEZUMA: (ignores his hand) No, vele la camisa. Es Americano. (Check out his shirt. He's American.)

LUIS: Me too...

Luis and Montezuma share a laugh.

MONTEZUMA: (to Mark) ...Hey.

Mark does not respond.

MONTEZUMA (CONT'D): Hey you!

MARK: Yeah?

LUIS: You a friend of Dick?

MARK: No.

MONTEZUMA: What are you reading?

MARK: Nothing good.

Mark puts the English to Spanish dictionary away.

LUIS: You new?

MARK: To what?

LUIS: (sarcastically to Montezuma) Oooh, *to what*.

MONTEZUMA: (to Mark) You know *what*.

MARK: No, I don't.

LUIS: You don't know?

MARK: Know what?

LUIS: I don't know.

MARK: What?

MONTEZUMA: (to Luis) I've never seen him around.

LUIS: Then you must be lost?

MARK: No.

MONTEZUMA: Are you a tourist?

MARK: No.

MONTEZUMA: What's the camera for?

LUIS: (to Mark) This ain't the zoo.

MONTEZUMA: You a newspaper man?

MARK: No.

MONTEZUMA: Pictures of me cost ten dollars.

LUIS: (to Montezuma) An artist or maybe an activist?

MARK: No --

MONTEZUMA: (to Mark) Are you an activist?

MARK: No.

MONTEZUMA: So...?

MARK: So...what?

LUIS: You waiting for the ice cream truck?

MARK: Yeah, I'm waiting for --

MONTEZUMA: For what?

MARK: What do you care. I don't need to tell you what I'm waiting for.

MONTEZUMA: No you don't.

MARK: What are you guys waiting for?

LUIS: *I'm,* waiting for some coffee.

MONTEZUMA: (to Mark) You waiting for coffee too?

MARK: No, I have some.

LUIS: If you're looking for some drugs --

MARK: I'm not --

LUIS: You need to go four blocks that way and look for some Puerto Ricans.

MARK: I'm --

LUIS: Just listen for the "*Mira -- Mira*".

MARK: I'm not looking for drugs.

MONTEZUMA: I'm not judging, but don't you think it's a little early for drugs.

MARK: I'm not --

LUIS: But if you go too far. You'll run into La Mara Salvatrucha (the MS-13), and those El Salvadorians will cut off your fingers and put them in your pockets.

MONTEZUMA: (to Luis) Why they do that?

LUIS: I think it's so you can't point them out.

MONTEZUMA: You think?

LUIS: What else could it be --

MARK: Thank you for the warning, but I'm fine. You, you guys fine?

LUIS: Como un coco recién nacido. ¿Tú? (Like a baby coconut. And you you?)

MARK: Huh?

LUIS: And you?

MARK: I didn't understand that --

MONTEZUMA: A baby coconut. Every morning we are like babies -- new to the world. Fresh.

MARK: Whatever you say.

A car horn is blasted accompanied by cheering from a passing car. The three watch the car drive by as we hear chants of "SI SE PUEDE (YES WE CAN)". Beat, long pause.

MONTEZUMA: (to Luis) ¿Hablaste con tu Primo? (Did you talk to your cousin?) --

LUIS: (to Mark) Hey, where are you from?

MARK: Why do you want to know?

LUIS: I'm just curious?

MARK: That's none of your business.

LUIS: I know...well?

MARK: Well what?

LUIS: What are you?

MARK: I'm an American.

MONTEZUMA: Me too. George Washington -- first president. Ahh...Betsy Ford made our flag. Ronald Reagan -- "Read my lips Mr. Gorbachev, take down these taxes!"

LUIS: (to Montezuma) Pendejo. (Asshole.)

MARK: You're a bit off --

MONTEZUMA: I bless my allegiance -- God pledge to America.

LUIS: (to Montezuma) It's a serious question.

MONTEZUMA: Of course.

LUIS: (to Mark) Where are you from?
MARK: I'm from New York -- Brooklyn. You?

LUIS: Me too.

MONTEZUMA: Luis -- (to Mark) Excuse me -- (to Luis) Hablaste con tu (Did you talk to your) --

LUIS: (to Mark)Where is your family from?

MARK: You mean originally?

LUIS: Yes.

MARK: Why do you want to know?

LUIS: I'm just making conversation.

MARK: For the most part I'm German-Irish, why?

LUIS: Just curious...and that's it?

MARK: Well, a little Native American and Russian --

LUIS: (to Montezuma) ¡Te lo dije! (I told you!)
(holding out his hand) ...Ten dollars.

MONTEZUMA: I didn't make a bet with you.

LUIS: We made a bet.

MONTEZUMA: No we didn't.

LUIS: We made a bet.

MONTEZUMA: Get out of here.

LUIS: (to Mark) Right, we made a bet.

MARK: I don't know.

MONTEZUMA: No bet was made.

LUIS: (pointing at the two) ...Sticking together I
see...you two could be cousins.

MONTEZUMA: (to Luis) I'm from Belarus and
you know that.

LUIS: Same thing.

MONTEZUMA: Really, my Guatemalan friend.

LUIS: That's not funny. You know I am a Mexicano (Mexican)
descended from Mayan kings.

MONTEZUMA: Oh, so it's not the same?

LUIS: No.

MONTEZUMA: Well then --

LUIS: (to Mark) I missed his point.

MONTEZUMA: (to Mark) The only thing he's
descended from is MYan ass -- (burst out in
laughter) ...Get it...my ass...

MARK: I missed it.

LUIS: (to Montezuma) Don't be a güey, güey
(jackass).

MONTEZUMA: Cabrón -- ¿Hablaste con tu primo? (Asshole -- did
you talk to your cousin?)

LUIS: ¿Cual? (Which one?)

MONTEZUMA: El Bellaco? (The Pervert?)

LUIS: ¿Del auto? (About the car?)

MONTEZUMA: Si. (Yes.)

Mark pulls out his English to Spanish dictionary and quickly glances
at it.

LUIS: Ya lo vendió. (he sold it.)

MONTEZUMA: ¿Cuando lo llamaste? (When did you call him?)

LUIS: El mismo dia. (The same day you asked.)

MONTEZUMA: ¡Mierda! (Bullshit!)

Luis notices Mark rifling through the dictionary, beat.

LUIS: Talk English. Your Spanish crucifies my ears anyway.

MONTEZUMA: Then speak my language...Mr. Teacher.

LUIS: Don't start. Just speak English.

MONTEZUMA: ¿Por que? (For what?)

LUIS: We don't want to be rude to our new neighbor.

MONTEZUMA: Que se joda (Screw) our neighbor.

LUIS: Ya, lo vendió.(clearly and slowly pronounced) My cou...sin al...ready...sold...the car.

MONTEZUMA: No seas puto. (Don't be a fag.)

LUIS: I told him that you were interested in the car the same day you asked.

MONTEZUMA: ¿Y lo vendió tan rápido? (And he sold it that fast?)

LUIS: Yes.

MONTEZUMA: Me fallaste, hombre (You let me down).
LUIS: Excuse me?

MONTEZUMA: (clearly and slowly pronounced) You fu...cked me.

LUIS: You owe me a coffee.

MONTEZUMA: Vete al carajo. (Go to hell.)

LUIS: (to Mark) Montezuma is a Spanish speaking Russian --

MONTEZUMA: Belarusian.

LUIS: So he likes to show off.

42

MARK: Good for him.

Beat. A car horn is blasted accompanied by cheering from a passing car. The three watch the car drive by as we hear chants of "SI SE PUEDE (YES WE CAN)".

LUIS: (toward the car) ¡Sí se pueden ir a la chingada! (Yes you can fuck off!)

MONTEZUMA: (to Luis) What's the matter with you?

LUIS: The noise is starting to bother me...and for what good is all that noise? You want me to march -- you pay me.

MONTEZUMA: You need some coffee.

LUIS: How can you be so calm? It's never been this long. Yesterday we sat around like pigeons.

MONTEZUMA: It'll pass.

LUIS: We need to maybe try something new.

MONTEZUMA: This is new. Give it time.

LUIS: We need to talk to Michigan. He won't listen to me -- but to all of us he would.

MONTEZUMA: Ehh... (to Mark) My friend, what's your name?

MARK: Mark.

MONTEZUMA: Montezuma. That over there is Luis.

MARK: Montezuma?

MONTEZUMA: That's what they call me. I'm a Spanish speaking Belarusian. Makes all the sense in the world, right.

MARK: What's your real name?

MONTEZUMA: Vladimir.

LUIS: I offered him Julio but he didn't like it.

MONTEZUMA: I like Montezuma. It sounds more heroic.

MARK: I guess.

MONTEZUMA: I have a gift for languages. I speak three.

LUIS: (sarcastically) A true Russian
philosopher.

MONTEZUMA: (to Mark) I lived and did
some work around South America when I was
younger.

LUIS: KGB.

MONTEZUMA: He's an idiot, don't listen to him.

LUIS: (pointing at Montezuma) ...An assassin.

MONTEZUMA: (to Mark) How many languages do
you speak?

MARK: English is all I need.

MONTEZUMA: Ahh...I would have to disagree.

MARK: I took some Spanish in high school but it didn't take.

MONTEZUMA: My father was one of the first in Cuba...you know,
back then.

MARK: Oh, yes.

MONTEZUMA: So, it's in the family.

Beat.

MARK: (to Luis) Where are you guys from originally?

LUIS: Me, New York.

MARK: Before that...your family.

LUIS: Nueva York.

MONTEZUMA: Me. A small village very far from Minske.

MARK: What's it called?

MONTEZUMA: Brooklyn.

MARK: Brooklyn?

MONTEZUMA: No, Brook...lyn.

MARK: You're kidding.

MONTEZUMA: No.

MARK: Yeah you are.

LUIS: I'm from there too -- generations.

MONTEZUMA: No he isn't.

MARK: Fine. You don't have to tell me. I was just curious...making conversation.

MONTEZUMA: He used to be a teacher.

LUIS: Don't start.

MONTEZUMA: (to Luis) History -- no?

LUIS: No.

MONTEZUMA: We call him Profesor (Professor), but he gets mad.

LUIS: I don't get mad.

MONTEZUMA: Well, we call him that when we *want* to get him mad.

LUIS: (to Mark) He really was an assassin.

MONTEZUMA: He got fired because he lied about history.

LUIS: His whole family, a bunch of assassins -- now Russian mob.

MONTEZUMA: Look at him now --

LUIS: His father shot Kennedy.

Michigan enters the playground. He carries a tool bag.

MICHIGAN: ¿Qué es esto? (What's this?)

He studies the repaired part of the fence.

LUIS: A fence.
MICHIGAN: Funny. This wasn't here yesterday.

MONTEZUMA: But today it is.

LUIS: (to Michigan) No coffee?

MICHIGAN: It's not my turn.

LUIS: I'm not brining you guys anymore coffee.

MICHIGAN: ¿Y (Where's) Marcelo?

LUIS: He didn't show up yet.

MICHIGAN: ¿Y ese -- quién es? (Who's this?)

LUIS: La muerte (Death).

MONTEZUMA: Tiene que ser un *hombre de minuto* (He has to be a *Minuteman*).

MICHIGAN: ¿En serio (Really)?

LUIS: Sí.

MICHIGAN: Como moscas sobre la mierda son éstos cabrones. (These assholes are like flies on shit.) ¿Hablaron con él? (Did you speak to him?)

MONTEZUMA: Nada más lo estábamos jodiendo un poquito. (Just fucking with him a little bit.)

LUIS: Ese cabrón (That fucker) Marcelo better show up with some coffee.

MONTEZUMA: Forget about the coffee, hombre (my man).

LUIS: I need my coffee.

MICHIGAN: (eyeing Mark) It must be nice to stand around and not have to worry about work --

LUIS: (to Montezuma) If I don't have my coffee it throws my whole day off.

MICHIGAN: (to Mark) Hey you!

Mark looks over his shoulder.

MICHIGAN (CONT'D): Yeah, you.

47

MARK: Can I help you.

MICHIGAN: The question is...how can I help you?

MARK: I don't need your help.

MICHIGAN: You sure?

MARK: Yes.

MICHIGAN: If you need help...we can help. You know...dry wall?
Cement? Cabinets, ceilings?

MONTEZUMA: Michigan, he don't need help like that.

MICHIGAN: (to Montezuma with a grin)
¿Trabajo? (Work?)

MONTEZUMA: No.

LUIS: It doesn't matter. We're not hiring anyway.

MARK: I'm waiting for the bus.

MICHIGAN: The bus don't stop here.

MARK: I meant, ride.

MONTEZUMA: You don't look like the bus riding type anyway.

MARK: We all need to conserve more.

LUIS: So you are a commuter?

MARK: Yup.

LUIS: (eyeing Mark) ...Very nice.

MARK: Global Warming --

LUIS: Y (And) El Niño y la Niña...son (are) motherfuckers.

MARK: I'm sorry?

LUIS: The weather, the ocean tides, you know.

MARK: Oh, yes.

LUIS: (to Mark) One time back home the river
swallowed my whole pueblito (town).

MARK: That must have been terrible.

LUIS: El Niño y la Niña.

MARK: If you say so.

LUIS: I do.

MICHIGAN: (starts to exit) Pues (Well), let me
go around --

MONTEZUMA: (to Michigan) Michigan, Me
and Luis were talking...and uh...have you
talked to Bengie?

MICHIGAN: Suave...

The day laborers step away from Mark. The repaired hole in the
fence clearly separates them.

MICHIGAN (CONT'D): Talk to Bengie for what?

MONTEZUMA: It's been over a week.

LUIS: And he had a lot of work.

MONTEZUMA: Ese boricua siempre tiene trabajo. (That Puerto
Rican always has work.)

MICHIGAN: If he needs us he'll come by.

MONTEZUMA: You said you were going to call him.

MICHIGAN: I changed my mind. He doesn't want us to call him.

LUIS: So then, are you sure Bengie knows we're here?

MICHIGAN: (eyeing Mark) ...So these fools
plan on following us to every new corner.

MONTEZUMA: (to Michigan) Forget about
our guest -- what about Bengie?

LUIS: Maybe he forgot that we moved.

MICHIGAN: I told him after our last job that we were moving here.
That things at the other corner were getting a little crowded and
filled with problems.

MONTEZUMA: It's never been this long.

MICHIGAN: I told all our regulars -- Anyway, Bengie has my
number.

LUIS: Over a week and not one job.

MICHIGAN: Luis, you can go back if you want. But we're better off
here, even with our gringo (white) friend.

LUIS: He's probably scared to risk it.

MICHIGAN: With all the work he has, he can't afford to be scared
for too long.

LUIS: With all the police and the news cameras at the raid, he could
be scared.

MICHIGAN: We'll be fine. And we're lucky we moved when we
did. God is on our side.

LUIS: I know, Peru Paco and his brother are in la pinta (prison) right now and probably will get deported. It's a big mess.

MONTEZUMA: (to Mark) Hey. Hey! Did you see that on the TV news?

MARK: What?

MONTEZUMA: The raid next to the Home Depot.

MARK: Uhh...no.

MICHIGAN: (to Luis) You see.

MONTEZUMA: They arrested a lot of people. It was a big story on the news.

MARK: What were they arrested for?

LUIS: It wasn't clear.

MARK: They must have been breaking the law.

MONTEZUMA: Depends.

MICHIGAN: (to Montezuma and Luis) Prosperity needs to continue...no? (to Luis) We're his best crew and he knows that.

LUIS: So you're sure you told him about our new spot?

MICHIGAN: Yes.

LUIS: And the others too?

MICHIGAN: Yes.

MONTEZUMA: And you gave him the right streets?

MICHIGAN: Yes.

Beat. A car horn is blasted accompanied by cheering from a passing car. They watch the car drive by as we hear chants of "SI SE PUEDE (YES WE CAN)".

MONTEZUMA: (to Michigan) So you're sure
you told him Hope Avenue, not street?
Because there is a Hope Street.

MICHIGAN: I know.

MONTEZUMA: Well?

MICHIGAN: It doesn't matter because I told him on the Corner of Hope and Haven. And Hope street, the one you are talking about doesn't cross Haven street.

MONTEZUMA: What?

LUIS: (to Montezuma) This is Hope Avenue
crossing Haven Street, entiendes (got it)?

MONTEZUMA: But what if Hope Street crosses Haven Street?

MICHIGAN: (thinking) ...I don't think that's
possible.

MONTEZUMA: Why...why you say that?

MICHIGAN: Because streets cross avenues not other streets.

MONTEZUMA: You sure?

LUIS: Sometimes they do.

MONTEZUMA: (to Mark) Do you know if
there's a Hope street?

MARK: Huh?

MONTEZUMA: Hope Street.

MARK: I don't know.

LUIS: So nobody knows.

MONTEZUMA: I'm pretty sure that I did some work at a Dairy Queen on a street called something like that.

MARK: Streets do usually cross Avenues --

MONTEZUMA: I tiled the whole place, I remember.

LUIS: A DQ?

MONTEZUMA: From front to back and the baseboards too.

LUIS: I think that is the right street. It was me and you. I did the ceiling work.

MONTEZUMA: It was Hope Street, right?

LUIS: I think so.

MONTEZUMA: Or was it Pope?

LUIS: Pope...like El Papa (The Pope)?

MONTEZUMA: I think.

MICHIGAN: It doesn't matter. He knows where we are. So we're fine.

LUIS: You sure?

MICHIGAN: Si (Yes).

MONTEZUMA: Now that I think of it, I think it's Hope Place not street?

LUIS: Okay -- ya (enough) -- con (with) the streets, courts, and avenues...

Montezuma paces in front of the phone.

MONTEZUMA: (more for himself) Bengie is running a business, sometimes the risk can get to high. He is waiting for things to cool down.

LUIS: I hope not too long. On the last job I gave Marcelo all the extra work.

MICHIGAN: (to Luis) He needed it.

LUIS: That hurt.

The pay phone rings.

MONTEZUMA: We all did what we had to.

MICHIGAN: (to Luis) He needed the money --

The pay phone rings. Mark crosses to answer it.

MICHIGAN (CONT'D): (to Mark) Hey, don't bother.

MARK: Why?

The pay phone rings.

MICHIGAN: It's not for you.

MARK: How would you know?

LUIS: I don't...but we don't use that phone.

MICHIGAN: Monte, the phone.

Montezuma picks it up and holds it out.

MONTEZUMA: (to Mark) It's a wrong number.

Montezuma hangs up the phone.

MICHIGAN: Montezuma!

MONTEZUMA: What?

MICHIGAN: Marcelo.

MONTEZUMA: Why would he call this phone.

LUIS: Not him, güey (dummy). He's expecting a call.

MONTEZUMA: I didn't know.

MARK: (to Michigan) Anyway, it's a public pay phone...so you have no right --

LUIS: (to Mark) It was probably bill collectors.

MARK: We'll never know now.

MICHIGAN: We're saving you from all the trouble. The last time we answered it...

Michigan calls Mark over.

MICHIGAN (CONT'D): I think it was the I.R.S.

MARK: (frustrated) Jesus.

We hear a cell phone ring. All three of the Day Laborers reach for their cell phones. Mark doesn't flinch. Michigan pulls out his cell phone and checks the caller I.D.

MICHIGAN: It's Marcelo... (to cell phone) Hola -- dime (Hello -- what's up)...Si, sigue aquí (Yes, he's still here)...A maricón... (burst into laughter)

Mark hears Michigan and glances over.

LUIS: El café. (The coffee.)

MICHIGAN: ¿Hablaste con Rosita? (Has Rosita called?)...No...Sonó el teléfono público (The public pay phone rang)...

MONTEZUMA: (gesturing with his hands emphatically) Michigan, no...it got disconnected.

MICHIGAN: ...Pero se colgó. (But it got disconnected.)...

LUIS: (to Michigan) El café. (The coffee.)

MICHIGAN: (to Luis) Hey, where was it that el Morenito (that black kid) was selling those phone cards?

LUIS: Outside Culito's Bodega.

MICHIGAN: He went there.

MONTEZUMA: Tell him to go check outside the Chinese place on Skillman and ahh...

LUIS: Heiser Street?

MONTEZUMA: Yeah, he might be there. (to Mark) Fifty dollar cards for ten dollars.

LUIS: (to Mark) No está mal. (Not bad.)

MICHIGAN: (to cell phone) Montezuma said to check the Chinese place on Skillman and Heiser.

LUIS: (to Michigan) Tell him to bring coffee --

MICHIGAN (to cell phone): Luis wants some -- hello?

LUIS: Coffee --

MICHIGAN: Bueno (Hello) --

LUIS: (throwing his hands in the air) ...There goes the coffee.

MICHIGAN: Se colgó. (It got disconnected.)

LUIS: Perfecto. (Perfect.)

Beat.

LUIS (CONT'D): (to Mark) So, you don't have a cell phone?

MARK: No.

LUIS: (to Mark) What type of operation are you guys running?

MARK: What do you mean?

LUIS: I don't know.

MARK: What?

MONTEZUMA: (sarcastically) Déjalo en paz. (Leave him alone.)

LUIS: (to Mark) Cell phones are pretty cheap now.

MARK: I know.

MICHIGAN: You don't even need a contract.

LUIS: (to Mark) You can even keep your number when you switch plans.

MARK: Mine was stolen.

LUIS: Really?

MARK: Out of my car.

LUIS: I always keep mine on me.

MARK: Well -- uh...that's a good idea.

MONTEZUMA: They make them very small now. You can carry them in your pocket --

MARK: Yeah, I know --

LUIS: Like gum.

MARK: What?

MONTEZUMA: Now with keys, phones, iPods, wallet, handkerchief --

LUIS: You carry a handkerchief?

MONTEZUMA: Yes. You?

LUIS: No.

MONTEZUMA: (to Mark) You?

MARK: No.

MONTEZUMA: Michigan?

MICHIGAN: ¿Para qué? (For what?)

MONTEZUMA: Hmmm. But anyway with all that stuff. It's like a man needs a purse.

LUIS: Maybe in Russia with all the puto (fag) ballet dancers.

MONTEZUMA: You know what I mean.

LUIS: No I don't.

MONTEZUMA: (to Michigan) Is everything okay with Marcelo?

MICHIGAN: His phone was running out of minutes and he's expecting a call.

LUIS: He hasn't heard from her yet?

Michigan gestures with his head that Luis step away from Mark. Montezuma follows. Mark tries to nonchalantly listen in. The repaired hole in the fence separates them.

MICHIGAN: No, and none of his family back home either. He's been on the phone with them all night.

MONTEZUMA: And he was expecting her today?

MICHIGAN: Yes.

LUIS: Is he sure that she left when she was supposed to?

MICHIGAN: Yes, he's been in contact with her twice a day since she crossed...until yesterday.

MONTEZUMA: Where was she the last time he talked to her?

MICHIGAN: I think in Tennessee.

LUIS: Not Tallahassee?

MICHIGAN: What?

LUIS: Florida (Spanish pronunciation).

MONTEZUMA: (to Luis) Why would she be in Florida. She's not on a tour.

LUIS: Did I say she is.

MICHIGAN: Why do you ask?

LUIS: Tennessee is closer.

MICHIGAN: He said Tennessee.

LUIS: Okay, good. (slapping Montezuma on the shoulder) Why didn't you answer the phone.

MONTEZUMA: I did.

LUIS: But you hung it up.

MONTEZUMA: I didn't know.

LUIS: Always clowning around. (to Mark) The Russian circus is always in town on this corner.

MICHIGAN: Okay ya (easy) --

MONTEZUMA: (to Luis) Why didn't you answer it.

LUIS: You were closer.

MICHIGAN: ¡Tiempo fuera! (Time out!)

MARK: I'm guessing one of us should have answered the phone.

MICHIGAN: Yes, but not you.

MARK: Well...some guy stopped by earlier and asked about the phone.

MICHIGAN: Who?

MARK: Some guy. He asked me if that phone had rang.

LUIS: Did it?

MARK: Not earlier. But, it did a minute ago.

LUIS: (to Michigan) Maybe it's her. You should
call him.

MICHIGAN: His phone has no minutes.

LUIS: Poor guy. It's scary. Anything could happen.

MICHIGAN: Just think good thoughts...and it will be fine.

MONTEZUMA: She's coming with their daughter too?

MICHIGAN: Yes.

LUIS: How old?

MICHIGAN: Eight. It's been eight years since he's seen her.

LUIS: It's a long time.

MONTEZUMA: His wife too.

Beat.

LUIS: I'm sure he's done his thing on the side.

MONTEZUMA: Who's talking about that?

MICHIGAN: Luis. Leave that alone.

LUIS: I'm sorry. But I knew this morning that today was going to be
a bad day.

MICHIGAN: The day has just started.

LUIS: Bengie can't find us...Marcelo's family is lost, and no coffee.

MONTEZUMA: Luis, relax.

LUIS: Last month I sent home half of what I usually send home.

MICHIGAN: You're not the only one.

LUIS: The very next day I get a call from my mother. They want to know if I'm okay.

MONTEZUMA: They worry.

LUIS: I know. It's my sister that drives me crazy...during the middle of the month she couldn't tell me from one day to another if my parents are even alive. But at the beginning of the month -- (trying to sound like his sister) "Hola, Mami." ("Hello, Mommy.")... (he pretends to receive money and counts it)

MICHIGAN: (sarcastically) You are not the only one with family we adore.

LUIS: You see. With out my coffee I'm an animal.

Beat.

MICHIGAN: (to Luis) Primo (Cousin), it will be fine.

LUIS: I hope.

MICHIGAN: Let me go around.

LUIS: Climb over, I'll catch you... (giggles)

MICHIGAN: I'll go around.

LUIS: No need. You can step through. Montezuma, help me.

Luis pulls on the repaired part of the fence. It gives a little.

MICHIGAN: I'll go around...

Montezuma helps Luis with the fence.

LUIS: You see. You can almost walk right through.

MICHIGAN: No exageres tanto. (No need to exaggerate.)

The fence gives a little more.

MARK: (more for himself) Hey guys. You
shouldn't do that.

LUIS: Michigan, your bag.

MARK: Just go around.

The fence gives a little more.

MARK (CONT'D): (looking around to see if anyone's watching) Hey
guys. That's public property you're destroying.

Michigan passes his bag through the fence. The fence gives a little
more.

LUIS: Ahora si (Here we go)...look, plenty of room to slide through.
They did ahh...how you always say, Montezuma? Shitty Work.

MONTEZUMA: Shoddy work, Americans always do shoddy
work...but shitty works too.

MARK: Hey...my taxes paid for this.

The day laborers freeze and all stare at Mark.

MICHIGAN: Maybe you paid for this, but I'm pretty sure the city
didn't.

63

MARK: You're ruining the security of the playground. This is why...

MONTEZUMA: Why what, amigo?

LUIS: This was ruined even after they finished fixing it.

MICHIGAN: Shoddy work.

MONTEZUMA: (to Mark) If you can't help...then please.

Michigan starts to shimmy through the fence. His shirt gets caught on a jagged part of the fence.

LUIS: (to Michigan) ¿Qué pasa, hombre? (What's up, man?)

MICHIGAN: Wait. I'm stuck.

MARK: (more for himself) You guys don't want me to call the police.

LUIS: (to Michigan) Move back.

MICHIGAN: Espérate. (Wait.) Don't push.

MONTEZUMA: (to Luis)Wait, it's caught on his shirt

Montezuma reaches in to help Michigan. Mark crosses toward the pay phone but pauses.

MARK: I'm calling the police.

Mark inches closer to the pay phone.

MICHIGAN: Oow -- oow!

Mark is startled, he stops.

LUIS: What?

MICHIGAN: My back.
LUIS: Ay Dios mio, viejo. (Oh Lord, old man.)

Michigan stops.

MICHIGAN: Wait, give me a minute.

MONTEZUMA: Be careful, it's going to tear your shirt (reaching in to unhook the shirt) -- Damn it!

Montezuma's sleeve gets caught on the fence.

MONTEZUMA (CONT'D): My sleeve is caught.

LUIS: You too?

MICHIGAN: Everyone wait one minute.

Beat.

MONTEZUMA: (starts to laugh) Hahaha...

LUIS: What's so funny?

MONTEZUMA: (laughing) ...Michigan...Stuck on the fence like the wet-back he is.

MICHIGAN: Fuck you --

LUIS: You're stuck too. Look at you, handcuffed to the fence.

MICHIGAN: I'm ready. Pull the fence more.

LUIS: I'm trying. A little help, Monte.

MONTEZUMA: I have one hand here. Let me get the other one free.

MARK: That was just fixed.

MONTEZUMA: It will be fine.

MARK: It's not fine.

LUIS: Why? Why is it not fine?

MARK: Look at it. Now it's broken.

The pay phone rings.

LUIS: The phone.

The pay phone rings.

MONTEZUMA: (to Luis) Pick it up.

The pay phone rings. Luis releases the fence, it digs into Michigan's stomach.

MICHIGAN: Oow! Pull it up!

Luis pulls the fence.

LUIS: Perdon (Sorry), Michigan.

The pay phone rings.

LUIS (CONT'D): Monte, the phone.

MONTEZUMA: I'm stuck too, animal (Spanish pronunciation).

The pay phone rings. Luis pulls on Montezuma's arm.

LUIS: Just pull it out.

MONTEZUMA: Oow! Wait, you're going to rip my shirt.

LUIS: Just pull it out, güey (jackass).

MONTEZUMA: It's caught.

The pay phone rings. The three look over at Mark.

MARK: Oh, it's okay now for me to answer the phone.

LUIS: If you could...please?

The pay phone rings. Beat, Mark answers the phone.

MARK: Hello.

LUIS: I bet you it's Rosita.

MARK: Hello.

Beat. Mark hangs up.

MICHIGAN: Who was it?

MARK: They hung up.

LUIS: It's because she heard a gringo (white boy).

MONTEZUMA: (to Luis) Don't be an idiot.

LUIS: Was it a woman's breathing?

MARK: I don't know.

MICHIGAN: Forget about that. Just get me out of here.

Luis pulls on the fence.

MONTEZUMA: Wait a minute.

Montezuma struggles to free his sleeve.

LUIS: (to Mark) Hey, Milton.

MARK: My name is Mark.

LUIS: Sorry.

MONTEZUMA: (to Luis) Pendejo. (Asshole.)
LUIS: (to Mark) Can you give us a hand
please? Before Michigan gets cut in half. I'm
no magician.

MONTEZUMA: Nor a very good plumber.

LUIS: (insulted) Really?

MONTEZUMA: Yes --

Luis shakes the fence.

MONTEZUMA (CONT'D): Oow!

MICHIGAN: Hey, hey!

MONTEZUMA (CONT'D): What the hell is a matter with you.

MICHIGAN: Luis, stop playing.

LUIS: (to Montezuma) I can make it so you
could never raise your middle finger at me
again.

MONTEZUMA: That hurt.

LUIS: You have anything else to say?

MONTEZUMA: You rip my shirt.

MICHIGAN: ¡Tiempo fuera! (Time out!)
(to Mark) Can you please give us a hand?

MARK: I'm not being part of that.

LUIS: I promise that I'll fix it.

MONTEZUMA: He's actually good with his hands.

MICHIGAN: He'll make it brand new.

MONTEZUMA: Okay, you're right. We should have gone around.

LUIS: (to Montezuma) Even though the
entrance to the playground is a 1/2 mile away –

MONTEZUMA: Luis, por favor (please)?

LUIS: I promise. I will make it brand new. That's what we do.

MONTEZUMA: We've learned our lesson.

Mark hesitantly crosses over and begins to help Montezuma.

MARK: Just please fix it.

LUIS: I will. I have some wire in my bag. That's what you guys
needed to do --

MARK: Just give me your word that you'll fix it.

LUIS: (stoically) My word is as good as oro
(gold).

MARK: I'll take that as a yes.

Mark frees Montezuma's sleeve.

MONTEZUMA: Thank you. (he checks his sleeve, to Luis) Look,
you ripped it.

LUIS: You can't even see that.

MONTEZUMA: I can see it.

LUIS: (to Montezuma) Help with the fence,
güey (man).

Montezuma does his best to help with the fence. Marcelo enters on
the street side of the fence.

MARCELO: What's going on here?

LUIS: Where the hell have you been?

MARCELO: I was getting a phone card --

LUIS: (to Marcelo) ¿Y el café? (And the coffee?)

MARCELO: It wasn't my turn.

Mark frees Michigan's shirt. He then pulls up on the fence.

MARK: (agitated) Alright, hurry up and slide
through...Christ.

MICHIGAN: Marcelo, give me a hand.

MARCELO: Why didn't you just go around.

LUIS: The entrance is like a mile away.

MARCELO: It's a block.

MICHIGAN: Marcelo, por favor (please). Nice and easy. My back.

MARCELO: Again. You need to have a doctor --

MONTEZUMA: I've told him.

MICHIGAN: I'm fine.

Marcelo grabs Michigan and helps him through the fence.

MICHIGAN (CONT'D): Ay-ay-ay (Oow oow
oow)...Gracias. Have you talk to Rosita?

MARCELO: No.

MICHIGAN: The pay phone just rang again.

MARCELO: It did.

The pay phone rings. Marcelo pushes Michigan out of the way. As Michigan falls in pain he accidently hits Luis in the crotch.

LUIS: Oow!

Luis quickly releases the fence and by accident smacks Mark in the face.

MARK: Ugh!

Luis doubles over grabbing his knees. Marcelo answers the phone.

MARCELO: Hello.

MONTEZUMA: (grabbing Mark by the shoulders)
...You Okay?

Toby enters. He sprints in with his can of pepper spray aimed and ready.

TOBY: Hey! Get off of --

MARK: Toby -- no!

Toby trips over a backpack on the ground, which causes him to spray the pepper spray. Luis and Mark take direct hits to the face.

LUIS: (covering his eyes) Ahhh!

MARK: (covering his eyes) Ahhh!

MONTEZUMA: (as he jumps away) Gas!

MARCELO: Hello.

MARK: (coughing) ...Toby, enough!

TOBY: (fumbling with the can of pepper spray) ...I'm
sorry! I didn't mean to --

LUIS: ¡Ayúdame, Virgen! (Help me, Mother of God!)

Montezuma tries to wrestle the can of pepper spray from Toby. They
fumble with it.

MARCELO: Hello!

TOBY: Sorry!

MONTEZUMA: Let go!

TOBY: You let go!

LUIS: (coughing) ...I can't breathe...

MARK: My eyes.

MARCELO: (to the guys) Shh, QUIET!

Everyone freezes.

MARCELO (CONT'D): (to pay phone)
Hello...No, there's no Julio here.

BLACK OUT:

SCENE THREE: EYE WASH

LIGHTS FADE UP:

Same day, same corner, one hour later. Mark sits on the wall to the right of the repaired part of the fence. Luis sits to the left of it. Marcelo sits a few feet away from Luis. He hangs his head. A few used water bottles are by their feet. It is obvious that they have washed their faces and rinsed their eyes out with the water.

LUIS: My eyes still feel like there melting.

MARK: Mine still burn a little too.

LUIS: You ever been maced before?

MARK: It was actually pepper spray.

LUIS: (sarcastically) Thanks for the clarification.

MARK: Anyway, One time.

LUIS: Why?

A car horn is blasted accompanied by cheering from a passing car. The three watch the car drive by as we hear chants of "SI SE PUEDE (YES WE CAN)".

LUIS (CONT'D): (to car) Ehh! Enough with the noise! It ain't going to change anything!

MARK: What's that about?

LUIS: The rally downtown.

MARCELO: They've been driving around making noise all morning.

MARK: I'm surprised you guys aren't there.

73

LUIS: You're not.

MARK: But if you were, then I probably would be.

LUIS: Siguiéndonos como un pedo pesado. (Following us around like a heavy fart.)

Marcelo chuckles.

MARK: Do I even want to know?

LUIS: (to Mark) What do you think came first...the rally or the raid.

MARK: Well in this case the raid, I would assume.

LUIS: Raid...rally, rally...raid. It's not going to change anything. Like Michigan likes to say, "prosperity needs to continue, no." And in this world prosperity goes to the cheapest labor, no.

Beat, awkward pause.

LUIS (CONT'D): Your friend was quite the vaquero (cowboy).

MARK: He was what?

LUIS: Cowboy.

MARK: He just misread the situation.

LUIS: He ran in here like fucking John Wayne. Shooting up the Indians.

MARK: Sorry about that. He's not a bad guy.

LUIS: He's a good friend of yours?

MARK: Not really. We used to work together.

LUIS: He took off to the store pretty quick once Montezuma started mentioning lawyers.

MARK: He sure did.

Marcelo stands and begins to pace.

LUIS: Marcelo, have a seat. Relax.

Marcelo checks to see if his cell phone has a signal. Luis does the same. The pay phone rings. Marcelo quickly picks it up.

MARCELO: Hello...hello?

LUIS: Is it her?

MARCELO: (to phone) I'm sorry I don't understand...I can't understand you. English...Inglés? I'm sorry, hello...Spanish -- Español?

Marcelo holds the phone out. Luis grabs it.

LUIS: Hello...we can't understand you...

The call is disconnected.

LUIS (CONT'D): Hello... (to Marcelo) They hung up.

MARCELO: It must have been a wrong number.

LUIS: It had to be.

MARK: For a phone that you guys don't use -- it's been pretty busy this morning.

Beat. Marcelo sits and hangs his head. The other two also sit in their respective spots. Beat.

LUIS: You have a girlfriend, Mark?

MARK: I'm married.

LUIS: That's nice.

MARK: If you say so.

LUIS: I do.

MARK: Why do you ask?

LUIS: Because if I did I would be home in bed with her right now...instead of being here with all of this mess.

MARK: She's at work.

LUIS: Oh...what does she do?

MARK: She's a first grade teacher.

LUIS: That's a good profession.

MARK: It is. She loves the kids.

LUIS: Do you have any kids?

MARK: No. Not yet.

LUIS: Why not? Kids are treasures.

MARK: You need to find a treasure to raise them in this City.

LUIS: It all balances out in the end, no?

MARK: (with Spanish inflection) No.

LUIS: I would disagree.

MARK: You married?

LUIS: No.

MARK: Do you have any kids?

LUIS: I have two boys. Ten and Twelve.

Luis proudly pulls out two worn and faded pictures from his wallet.

MARK: Must be hard...uh, they with their mother?

LUIS: She died a few years ago. Now they're with their grandmother -- my mother.

MARK: I'm sorry to hear that.

LUIS: I'm not. She was an awful woman. The kind of woman that is never satisfied, you know.

MARK: (unsure) Kind of.

LUIS: The kind that lives angry because they think they had to settle.

MARK: We all are forced to settle in some way.

LUIS: You think?

MARK: Yup.

Luis turns to the fence and tugs on the repaired part.

LUIS: ...I guess you're right. I'm here because of her.

MARK: Were you really a teacher?

LUIS: (smirks) ...Hmm...Montezuma is a funny guy, a trouble maker.

MARK: It's been an interesting morning.

LUIS: Teaching is a honorable profession.

Mark agrees, beat.

MARK: ...My wife really does love it. Trying to make the kids better, you know. She's a great girl...good heart. I'm lucky to have her.

MARCELO: A man needs his family...a good woman by his side, tú mujer, (woman) to make him good too.

LUIS: If you're so lucky.

Beat, awkward pause.

LUIS (CONT'D): Who needs coffee?

MARCELO: What I need is un guaro fuerte (a strong shot).

LUIS: A little early.

MARCELO: Not today.

LUIS: I'm going to go get coffee.

MARCELO: I'll take one.

LUIS: Black?

MARCELO: Si. (Yes.)

LUIS: (to Mark) Would you like something?

MARK: Toby and the guys should be right back.

LUIS: They'll forget.

MARCELO: Luis, I'll go.

LUIS: You sure?

MARCELO: I need to take a walk.

LUIS: That will be good for you. Milk, two sugar.

MARCELO: (to Mark) Would you like a coffee?

MARK: I'm fine, thank you.

LUIS: (reaching in his pocket) ...Here, let me --

MARCELO: I got it. I think it was my turn anyway.

LUIS: You sure you don't want me to go?

MARCELO: I'll be right back...just answer the pay phone if it rings.

LUIS: We will.

MARCELO: I'll be right down the block. I'll be fast.

LUIS: Don't worry. Take your time.

Marcelo exits. Beat.

LUIS (CONT'D): Why would you spend your day off here? I'm
sure there are more important things you could be doing. Maybe
making some money -- overtime.

MARK: I'm laid-off right now.

LUIS: Oh, I'm sorry.

MARK: I'm collecting.

LUIS: Collecting...that's nice.

MARK: Anyway, uhh...instead of being home with my thumb up
my ass, I thought I would do my part.

LUIS: Do your part?

MARK: Yeah.

LUIS: Volunteer at a shelter -- feed the poor.

MARK: The poor get enough help. What about the working man.

LUIS: You have a point there.
MARK: You telling me.

Beat.

MARK (CONT'D): I guess I could be finishing tiling
the bathroom. The wife hated the old color.

LUIS: That's a good days work.

MARK: Day. I've been at it for a few days now. It's a pain in the ass.

LUIS: You just have to be patient with it.

MARK: Let's just say that I wasn't born with the carpentry gene.

LUIS: It's a skill.

MARK: I didn't measure it right so it wasn't centered.

LUIS: You should take one of those classes at Home Depot.

MARK: I'll figure it out. Once I get the right tools to cut and space it
out, I'll be fine.

LUIS: You could hire me but I don't think you could afford me
right now.

The two share an uneasy laugh, beat.

LUIS (CONT'D): What do you do? When you're doing it.

MARK: I'm in manufacturing.

LUIS: What kind?

MARK: I make electrical harnesses for the aviation industry.

LUIS: Military?

MARK: No...for the most part our stuff is for commercial airlines.

LUIS: Any specific airline?

MARK: No. Why?

LUIS: Because I would think twice before I flew with them.

MARK: Funny.

LUIS: I probably would rather walk.

MARK: I'm sure you've done plenty of that.

LUIS: I've done my share.

MARK: I'm sure you didn't fly in.

LUIS: Walking is part of life. Just like standing in an unemployment line, no?

MARK: Shouldn't have to be.

Beat.

MARK (CONT'D): On a good day how much you guys bring in?

LUIS: It depends on the work -- but anything is always better than nothing.

MARK: I guess that depends, don't it? I mean...busting your ass all day for pennies gets you what?

LUIS: Eventually closer to the next dollar.

MARK: That sounds nice but --

LUIS: Mark, why are you here? On this corner with me. I have no idea on how to make electrical harnesses for airplanes.

MARK: Well, it's bigger than that.

LUIS: And it's pretty clear that you don't know how to tile a floor. We shouldn't be enemies.

MARK: I don't see us as enemies.

LUIS: You don't?

MARK: No, not really.

LUIS: I'm just here trying to make my pennies so my kids can live better.

MARK: I ain't against that.

LUIS: That's why *I'm* here on this corner.

MARK: Good for you.

LUIS: But why are *you* here on this corner?

MARK: I just want to work too, and not have to worry about losing my job to people who don't have the right to be here. That's all I'm saying.

LUIS: Mark, no law or fence will ever stop a man from an opportunity to work toward a better life for his family.

MARK: You guys...you take the money but what do you give back.

LUIS: We give back to this country every day.

MARK: It's because of you that skilled blue collar guys, like me, lose work.

LUIS: Like I said, I know nothing about electrical harnesses.

MARK: You know it's more complicated than that.

LUIS: All I know is that it's my cheap labor that pours those cement floors you guys work on.

MARK: Exactly, it's you guys that drive down wages.

LUIS: Isn't that American free enterprise at its best.

MARK: You see. You don't even love this country.

LUIS: I love my family -- does that make me a criminal?

MARK: What are you talking about? I never called you that.

LUIS: I'm sure your Minutemen say we are. But those same people you call criminals, risk their lives every day for a chance of a better life for their family. When's the last time you've done the same.

MARK: That's why I love this country because I don't have to risk my life.

LUIS: So good it is to be lucky.

Michigan, Montezuma, and Toby enter carrying a couple small black plastic bags filled with breakfast sandwiches, a twelve pack of Corona bottles, and a large Duane Reade bag stuffed with snacks, drinks, and some first aid supplies.

MONTEZUMA: Profesor (Spanish pronunciation)! We made a run to the pharmacy. We picked up a couple of those heat pads for Michigan's back.

LUIS: (to Montezuma) About time you got back.

Michigan shows off a couple heat patches on his lower back.

TOBY: Those things work great. I use them all the time.

MICHIGAN: They feel good.

Without much effort the men take their respective sides on the sidewalk.

LUIS: The coffee?

MICHIGAN: Ahh...

LUIS: I knew you guys would forget.

MONTEZUMA: Forget about the coffee... (holding up case of beer) ...we have something better now.

The repaired hole in the fence divides the men again.

TOBY: Alright, Mark, I have to head out.

MARK: Okay, umm...

MONTEZUMA: (sarcastically) Bye, Toby. And thank you for all this great stuff.

TOBY: I'm really sorry about the miss understanding. I didn't mean to spray you guys.

LUIS: Yes, we know.

MICHIGAN: Don't worry about it.

TOBY: Enjoy the rest of the day.

LUIS: We'll try -- OOW... (covering his eyes) ...I'm just kidding.

TOBY: Again, I'm really sorry. I jumped the gun. We're cool, right?

MONTEZUMA: Of course my new friend.

TOBY: Have a good night guys. (to Michigan) Be sure to use that Epsom Salt tonight.

MICHIGAN: I will.

Toby throws his arm around Mark.

TOBY: Hey, walk with me.

The two cross to the edge of the stage.

TRANSITION LIGHTS:

Lights dim over the day laborers.

TOBY (CONT'D): (a bit panicked) Dude, you have to hang out here and make sure things are smoothed over.

MARK: Okay, sure.

TOBY: I mean...I bought them all that stuff so I should be good. But, I can't have some lawyer calling my house. My wife would kill me.

MARK: She's never going to find out.

TOBY: The fucking Russian guy was talking lawyers --

MARK: It'll be fine.

TOBY: No cops -- nothing.

MARK: Toby --

TOBY: She didn't want me to buy the truck, okay. We're housing hunting -- she said it was too much...

MARK: Take it easy --

TOBY: Her dad let me borrow the money. And it's not new, it's pre-owned.

MARK: Toby, listen to me.

TOBY: She'd leave me, man.

MARK: No she wouldn't.

TOBY: She would.

MARK: It'll be fine.

TOBY: We're trying to close on a house in Jersey. I can't be getting sued by the A.C.L.U. or the fucking La Raza, do you understand.

MARK: I'm sure everything will be fine.

TOBY: The media eats that type of shit up. (in air quotes) The victimized illegal --

MARK: And now assaulted.

TOBY: Shit...what's from stopping them from calling the police tomorrow.

MARK: Relax.

TOBY: That's why they come up here. Trying to find that lottery ticket. I'm not trying to be no lottery ticket. Especially not to some fence hopping Mexican.

MARK: I'll hang out a little longer. It'll be fine. I got something I need to take care of anyway.

TOBY: Yeah, hang out and try infiltrating a little bit to see what they're thinking, you know. Like what you were talking about earlier this morning.

MARK: Sure.

TOBY: And tomorrow we'll try another corner. Let this one be for a little bit.

MARK: Whatever you think is best.

TOBY: There some Haitians out in East Flatbush that can use a *presence*, you know. Or some Chinese in Flushing.

MARK: Okay. I'll call you later tonight.

TOBY: Let's do that, let's talk tonight...Oh yeah. I got something for you in the truck.

They exit.

TRANSITION LIGHTS:

Lights up full over the day laborers.

LUIS: (rifling through the bag) ...It looks like you guys went on a shopping spree.

MONTEZUMA: You should have seen him. He couldn't stop apologizing. He really believed that I was going to call my lawyer.

LUIS: What lawyer.

MONTEZUMA: I told him I was going to call *La Raza*.

LUIS: You're Russian.

MONTEZUMA: Belarusian...

They share a laugh. Mark enters. He hesitantly carries a brand new holstered can of pepper spray.

LUIS: Ay mira (Oh look), John Wayne Junior.

MONTEZUMA: (throwing up his hands)
...Don't shoot.

87

The day laborers share a laugh.

MARK: (sarcastically) Ha-ha-ha.

MICHIGAN: I say we call it a day -- go drink our beer.

MONTEZUMA: That sounds good to me. What's better than a nice buzz before lunch time.

LUIS: A morning siesta sounds good.

MARK: Hey guys, Toby was really sorry about what happened. It's not supposed to get that personal -- people getting hurt.

MICHIGAN: What if that was a gun.

MONTEZUMA: He would of shot Luis in the eye, me in the mouth, and himself in the balls.

MARK: He really was sorry to bother you with all of that.

LUIS: He should be.

MARK: He really, really is. We'll be sure not to *bother* you guys with that again.

LUIS: Okay.

MONTEZUMA: It's good to hear.

LUIS: Siesta time!

MICHIGAN: Y (where's) Marcelo.

LUIS: He went for a walk. He needed it.

MICHIGAN: Which way did he go?

LUIS: (pointing off stage) That way.

MICHIGAN: Good, let's go find him.

LUIS: What about the pay phone?

MICHIGAN: He got minutes for his phone.

LUIS: He told me to answer it if it rang.

MICHIGAN: I'm sure he wasn't planning on standing here all day and night.

MONTEZUMA: Well go find him, and if he wants to come back we'll come back.

MICHIGAN: (to Luis) Okay?

LUIS: You're the boss.

MICHIGAN: Come on, well go to Pepino's Bodega.

The day laborers gather their things.

MICHIGAN (CONT'D): I'm sure Doña Carmen will let us drink in the back.

MONTEZUMA: Sure, as long as we buy something, take off our shoes, and share the beer.

MICHIGAN: You know what, Montezuma. I think you have something for Doña Carmen.

MONTEZUMA: Have some respect, Michigan.

LUIS: (to Mark) You interested in a beer?

MONTEZUMA: On Toby.

LUIS: We can finish our talk.

MARK: I don't think so.

LUIS: Until we meet again.

The day laborers start to exit. Mark tugs on the fence.

MARK: (to Luis) The fence.

LUIS: What about it?

MARK: (to Luis) You ready to fix it.

LUIS: Don't worry about it. I'll get to it.

MARK: You gave me your word that you would fix it.

LUIS: I will.

MARK: I'll sleep better if I know it's done. I'll help you.

Luis turns to Montezuma and Michigan. They shrug their shoulders.

LUIS: (to Mark) Let's get to work.

Luis crosses toward the hole in the fence.

MICHIGAN: Pues, nos vemos alla. (Well, We'll see you over there.)

LUIS: Pepino's?

MICHIGAN: Sí. (Yes.)

Michigan and Montezuma start to exit.

MONTEZUMA: (to Luis) Have fun with your
new apprentice... (giggles)

The pay phone rings.

LUIS: Michigan, the phone.

Michigan answers the phone.

MICHIGAN: Hello...Bueno...Rosita...¿Es usted? (is it you?)

LUIS: ¿Rosita?

MICHIGAN: No llore. (Don't cry.) Soy amigo de (I'm a friend of) Marcelo.

LUIS: Where is she?

MONTEZUMA: (to Luis) Shh.

MICHIGAN: (to the pay phone) Rosita, deme
un minuto por favor. (give me a minute
please.)
(to the guys as he covers the phone) ¡Busquen a (Go
find) Marcelo!

LUIS: He went to go get coffee down the block.

MONTEZUMA: I thought you said he went for a walk.

LUIS: He went for both.

MICHIGAN: Hey, it doesn't matter.

MONTEZUMA: (to Luis) You made him go get
coffee.

LUIS: No, he wanted to go.

MONTEZUMA: You're unbelievable.

LUIS: He wanted to go.

MICHIGAN: ¡Atención, imbéciles! (Give me your attention,
imbeciles!) --

LUIS: Right, Mark? He wanted to go.

MARK: He did.

MICHIGAN: Go find him.

LUIS: (pointing off stage) ...He only went down the block.

MICHIGAN: Go get him.

MONTEZUMA: (looking off stage) ...There he is.

LUIS: ¡Marcelo!

Luis waves him down.

LUIS (CONT'D): ¡It's Rosita! Rosita!

MONTEZUMA: ¡Apúrate, hombre! (Hurry up, man!)

Marcelo enters. He dashes in carrying a full cardboard tray of coffee and a stack of lottery scratch-off tickets.

MARCELO: Rosita?

MICHIGAN: (holding out phone) Si. (Yes.)

Luis reaches for the tray of coffee. Not even thinking of the coffee Marcelo tosses the whole tray in the trash and grabs the phone. He hangs onto the lottery scratch-off tickets.

MARCELO: Rosita...Ay, Rosa...¿Que paso? (What happened?)

LUIS: (to Michigan) She was crying?

MARCELO: ¿Están bien? (Are you okay?)

MICHIGAN: Yes. She sounded scared.

MARK: (quietly to Luis) What's going on?

Luis shrugs him off.

MARCELO: (to pay phone) ¿Y la nena? (And the girl?)...

MONTEZUMA: At least now he's heard from her.

MARCELO: (starts to break down, covers his face with his free hand) Ay, perdóname (forgive me), Rosa. Perdóname (Forgive me) Elliana -- hija (daughter)...

MICHIGAN: (grabbing Marcelo by the arm) Where is she?

MARCELO: (crying) ...They robbed her.

MONTEZUMA: Is she okay?

MARCELO: (to pay phone) No llores, mi amor. (Don't cry, my love.)
(to the guys) They put her on a bus and took everything else. Le robaron hasta el anillo. (They even took her wedding ring).

MICHIGAN: ¿Pero está bien? (Is she okay?)

MARCELO: Sí, gracias a Dios. (Yes, thank God.)
(to pay phone) Rosita, cálmate (be calm)...
Llegaste, mi amor (You made it)...
lo hiciste. (You did it.)...
Pon a la nena (Put my baby on)...
Bendicion, mi cariño (God bless you, my darling)...
Sí estás en los Estado Unidos

(Yes you're in the United State)...
Nos vemos pronto, cariño
(Very soon, we will see each other).

MICHIGAN: (more urgent) Where is she?

MARCELO: (to pay phone) Cariño, pon a tu
mamá...Rosita, ¿Donde estás? (Where are you?)

MONTEZUMA: Find out where she is and we'll go get them.

LUIS: Esos malditos coyotes son ladrones -- animales (Those damn
coyotes are thieves -- animals).

MARCELO: (to the group) She says she's in
New York City.

LUIS: Is she sure she's in Manhattan?

MARCELO: (to pay phone) Cálmate, mi amor
(Calm down, my love)...¿Qué ves? (What do
you see?)

MICHIGAN: Tell her to ask someone.

LUIS: Tell her to look for someone Latino.

MARCELO: Shh.

MONTEZUMA: Let the man listen.

MARCELO: (listening to pay phone) ...She says
they're at a bus station.

LUIS: That won't help.

MONTEZUMA: (to Luis) Relax, hombre (man).

LUIS (to Marcelo): Where was she supposed to get
dropped off?

MARCELO: They were supposed to call us.

MICHIGAN: Tell her to look around. What does she see?

MONTEZUMA: She has to be at Penn or the Port Authority --

LUIS: Maybe she's in Jersey.

MARCELO: (as he listens to pay phone) ...She's
under a bridge.

LUIS: The Brooklyn Bridge?

MONTEZUMA: She's coming from the other direction you idiot.

LUIS: Maybe they took a tunnel and were headed to Brooklyn --

MONTEZUMA: (to Luis) Ahh. (to Marcelo) Tell her
to ask somebody.

LUIS: A Latino!

MARCELO: (to pay phone) Mi amor,
pregúntale a alguien. (My love, ask somebody.)

LUIS: If she's in the City, every other person will speak Spanish,
no?

MONTEZUMA: Tell her to walk into a negocio (business), a
restaurant -- to the kitchen.

MARCELO: (as he listens to pay phone) ...she's
asking somebody...Washington Heights!

MARK: The George Washington Bridge.

LUIS: Está con los Dominicanos (She's with the Dominicans).

MARK: There's a bus station under the bridge.

MICHIGAN: Marcelo, nos vamos en un (we'll take a) taxi. Tell her not to move.

MARCELO: (to pay phone) Mi amor...

Marcelo turns his back to the audience as he carries an unheard conversation on the phone.

LUIS: (to Michigan) That's going to be expensive...from Queens to Washington Heights.

MICHIGAN: How much you think?

LUIS: Forty including tip...maybe.

Marcelo hangs up the phone.

MARCELO: She's waiting for us inside. Una China saw her crying by a pay phone in the bus station. Who knows how they communicated.

LUIS: But that bus station should be filled with Dominicans.

MONTEZUMA: She's new here. She's probably scared out of her mind.

LUIS: (agitated) Es que esos Dominicanos son malos (It's because those Dominicans are bad).

MARCELO: (to Michigan) I should have gone for her.

MICHIGAN: Let's get a taxi.

Michigan pulls out some money from his pocket.

MICHIGAN (CONT'D): I have sixteen and some change...

(as he gathers and counts his change) ...Marcelo, how
much money do you have?

The rest of the guys dig into their pockets, except for Mark.

MARCELO: Doce (Twelve).

MICHIGAN: Eighteen con los (with the) pennies.

MONTEZUMA: I have three dollars.

LUIS: That's it?

MARCELO: I should have never bought those lottery tickets.

MONTEZUMA: (to Luis) And you?

LUIS: (still searching his pockets) ...It wasn't my turn
for the coffee so I didn't bring a lot of money. I
bought a newspaper and a pack of gum...so all I have
is...(counting the change) ...Four dollars and ten
cents.

MICHIGAN: How much is that?

MARCELO: Thirty seven dollars and...

LUIS: Ten cents.

MONTEZUMA: That will have to do.

Mark reaches into his pockets and pulls out some money.

MARK: (counts the money) ...I have two ninety
you can have.

Mark hands Marcelo the money.

MARCELO: Gracias (Thank you).

LUIS: Thank you.

Marcelo shoves the lottery scratch-off tickets into Mark's chest. Mark takes them.

MARCELO: Pues (Well), let's go.

MONTEZUMA: First we need a cab -- there's one. (throwing up his arms) Hey!

The cab drives by.

MONTEZUMA (CONT'D): You bastard!

MICHIGAN: There's another one. (exiting) Taxi, over here!

MONTEZUMA: He got it.

Michigan enters.

MICHIGAN: Apúrense. (Hurry.)

Marcelo, Montezuma and Michigan quickly gather their things.

LUIS: Ándale. (Get going.)

MARCELO: Vamonos. (Let's go.)

Marcelo and Michigan exit.

MONTEZUMA : Nos vemos. (See you later.)

Montezuma leaves the case of beer with Luis.

MONTEZUMA (CONT'D): Para la sed. (For your thirst.)

LUIS: Gracias. (Thanks.) Call me.

Montezuma exits. They watch the cab drive away, beat. They both turn and study the fence.

LUIS (CONT'D): Would you like a beer?

MARK: Sure why not.

Luis pulls out two beers. He cracks the beers and hands one to Mark.

MARK (CONT'D): I'm sure his wife and kid are fine.

Luis takes a swig of beer.

LUIS: (studying Mark) ...A little warm.

Mark takes a swig of beer.

MARK: I've had worse. You know...we should cover these up.

Mark pulls two paper bags out of the trash. He uses them to cover the beers.

MARK (CONT'D): This will work.

LUIS: No one would ever suspect.

Luis pulls out some wire and pliers from his bag.

LUIS (CONT'D): Strange day.

MARK: You never know what the sun will bring.

LUIS: It could have been worse.

MARK: I guess it always can.

They start repairing the fence. They work well together.

LUIS: I'll start at the top and you at the bottom.

MARK: Alright.

LUIS: Anchor the end. Twist it real tight. And pull the wire through.

MARK: Through every link?

LUIS: Every other link is good.

MARK: You sure?

LUIS: Yeah. Just pull it tight.

MARK: You guys do fences too?

LUIS: Not really. But we're good in getting through them.

They share a laugh.

LUIS (CONT'D): There.

They finish the repair.

LUIS (CONT'D): Brand new.

MARK: Looks good.

Luis tugs on the fence.

LUIS: Not even a tigre (tiger) can get through that fence.

MARK: (sarcastically) How about a Mexican?

They share a laugh.

LUIS: Not even a Mexican. But a Guatemalan, maybe.

They share a laugh. They both admire their work.

LUIS (CONT'D): Tomorrow?

MARK: I'm not sure.

LUIS: Me. Yes.

MARK: Well then...I should go...thanks for the fence.

LUIS: That's what we do -- make things brand new.

MARK: Not quite new but it'll do the job.

LUIS: Si. (Yes.)

MARK: You staying?

LUIS: I'm going to finish my beer. And then like Michigan said, "Call it a day." I'll take it as a...half day -- a personal, you know.

MARK: (with a chuckle) ...Yeah, yeah...Which way you heading out?

Mark pulls out a set of car keys from his pocket.

LUIS: (motioning with his head) I go that way. On my two sturdy feet.

MARK: (referring to the opposite direction with his head) Oh...I'm going that way.

LUIS: I'm not the one who needed a ride, güey (my friend).

MARK: That's not why I asked.

LUIS: Oh...

MARK: Well...Here... (hands Luis a lottery scratch-off ticket)

LUIS: Oh...

MARK: Maybe you'll get paid for your work.

LUIS: Maybe you too.

MARK: (holding up the lottery tickets) ...Good luck.

Mark tosses his beer away, he exits. Luis gathers his things as he finishes his beer. He begins to exit. "Beep - Beep", Luis looks over.

The pay phone rings. Luis quickly answers the pay phone.

LUIS : ...Hello...hello...no, there's no Aasim here.

Luis hangs up the phone.

BLACK OUT: END OF PLAY.

NoPassport
Press

NoPassport is an unincorporated theatre alliance devoted to cross-cultural, Pan-American performance, theory, action, advocacy, and publication.

NoPassport Press c/o PO Box 1786, South Gate CA 90280 USA e-mail: NoPassportPress@aol.com

Dreaming the Americas Series

Antigone Project: A Play in Five Parts
by Tanya Barfield, Karen Hartman, Chiori Miyagawa, Lynn Nottage and Caridad Svich, with Preface by Lisa Schlesinger, Introduction by Marianne McDonald. **ISBN 978-0-578-03150-7**

Elaine Avila: Jane Austen, Action Figure and other plays
Preface by Ted Gregory, afterword by Kathleen Weiss.
ISBN: 978-0-578-10420-1

Kia Corthron: A Cool Dip in the Barren Saharan Crick and other Plays
(A Cool Dip...Light Raise the Roof, Tap the Leopard) Preface by Michael John Garces, Interview by Kara Lee Corthron. **ISBN: 978-0-578-09749-7**

Amparo Garcia-Crow: The South Texas Plays
(Cocks Have Claws and Wings to Fly, Under a Western Sky, The Faraway Nearby, Esmeralda Blue) with Preface by Octavio Solis. **ISBN: 978-0-578-01913-0**

Migdalia Cruz: El Grito del Bronx & other plays
(Salt, Yellow Eyes, El Grito del Bronx, Da Bronx rocks: a song)
Introduction by Alberto Sandoval-Sanchez, afterword by Priscilla Page.
ISBN: 978-0-578-04992-2

Envisioning the Americas: Latina/o Theatre & Performance
A NoPassport Press Sampler with works by Migdalia Cruz, John Jesurun, Oliver Mayer, Alejandro Morales and Anne Garcia-Romero
Preface by Jose Rivera. Introduction by Caridad Svich
ISBN: 978-0-578-08274-5

Catherine Filloux: Dog and Wolf & Killing the Boss
Introduction by Cynthia E. Cohen. **ISBN: 978-0-578-07898-4**

David Greenspan: Four Plays and a Monologue
(Jack, 2 Samuel Etc, Old Comedy, Only Beauty, A Playwright's Monologue)
Preface by Helen Shaw, Introduction by Taylor Mac, **ISBN: 978-0-578-08448-0**

103

Karen Hartman: Girl Under Grain
Introduction by Jean Randich. **ISBN: 978-0-578-04981-6**

Kara Hartzler: No Roosters in the Desert
Based on field work by Anna Ochoa O'Leary **ISBN: 978-0-578-07047-6**

John Jesurun: Deep Sleep, White Water, Black Maria – A Media Trilogy
Preface by Fiona Templeton. **ISBN: 978-0-578-02602-2**

Carson Kreitzer: SELF DEFENSE and other Plays
Self Defense, The Love Song of J Robert Oppenheimer, 1:23, Slither)
Preface by Mark Wing-Davey, Introduction by Mead K. Hunter.
ISBN: 978-0-578-08058-1.

Lorca: Six Major Plays: *(Blood Wedding, Dona Rosita, The House of Bernarda Alba, The Public, The Shoemaker's Prodigious Wife, Yerma)*
In new translations by Caridad Svich, Preface by James Leverett,
Introduction by Amy Rogoway. **ISBN: 978-0-578-00221-7**

Matthew Maguire: Three Plays: *(The Tower, Luscious Music, The Desert)* with Preface by Naomi
Wallace. **ISBN: 978-0-578-00856-1**

Oliver Mayer: Collected Plays: *(Conjunto, Joe Louis Blues, Ragged Time)*
Preface by Luis Alfaro, Introduction by Jon D. Rossini
ISBN: 978-0-6151-8370-1

Chiori Miyagawa: America Dreaming and other Plays
Preface by Emily Morse, Afterward by Martin Harries
ISBN: 978-0-578-10189-7

Chiori Miyagawa: Woman Killer
introduction by Sharon Friedman, afterword by Martin Harries
ISBN: 978-0-578-05008-9

Alejandro Morales: Collected Plays: *(expat/inferno, marea, Sebastian)*
ISBN: 978-0-6151-8621-4

Popular Forms for a Radical Theatre
Edited by Caridad Svich and Sarah Ruhl
ISBN: 978-0-578-09809-8

Lisa Ramirez: EXIT CUCKOO (Nanny in motherland)
ISBN: 975-0-578-07520-4.

Anne Garcia-Romero: Collected Plays:
(Earthquake Chica, Santa Concepcion, Mary Peabody in Cuba)
Preface by Juliette Carrillo. **ISBN: 978-0-6151-8888-1**

<u>Octavio Solis: The River Plays</u> *(El Otro, Dreamlandia, Bethlehem)*
Introduction by Douglas Langworthy. **ISBN: 978-0-578-04881-9**

<u>Saviana Stanescu: The New York Plays</u>
(Waxing West, Lenin's Shoe, Aliens with Extraordinary Skills)
Introduction by John Clinton Eisner. **ISBN: 978-0-578-04942-7**

<u>12 Ophelias (a play with broken songs)</u> by Caridad Svich
ISBN: 978-0-6152-4918-6 *(theatre & performance text series single edition)*

<u>The Tropic of X</u> by Caridad Svich
Introduction by Marvin Carlson, Afterword by Tamara Underiner
ISBN: 978-0-578-03871-1

<u>NoPassport Press "Dreaming the Americas" print-on-demand series</u>
<u>Series Editors:</u> Jorge Huerta, Mead K. Hunter, Randy Gener, Otis Ramsey-Zoe, Stephen Squibb, Caridad Svich

Made in the USA
Las Vegas, NV
09 January 2024

84132797R00065